Bob's Birthday Celebration!

EGMONT

We bring stories to life

This edition published in Great Britain 2009 by Egmont UK Limited
239 Kensington High Street, London W8 6SA

ISBN 978 0 6035 6472 7
1 3 5 7 9 10 8 6 4 2
Printed in China

"Listen, everybody!" Wendy exclaimed. "Today is Bob's birthday. Let's pretend it's just an ordinary day and surprise Bob with a party this afternoon!"

"Won't Bob be disappointed if we don't wish him a happy birthday?" asked Muck.

"We can wish him a happy birthday at the party," Wendy explained. "Now remember, it's a secret. Not a word to Bob!"

Just then, Bob came into the yard.

"Hi, Wendy. Was there any post for me?" he asked.

"Were you expecting anything special?" she teased.

"Uh . . . no. Nothing special," he said.
Bob turned to Scoop and Lofty. "We have to fix Farmer Pickles' barn."

"Have a good day, Bob," Wendy called.

"I'll try," mumbled Bob as he left the yard with Scoop and Lofty.

"Now I can begin baking Bob's birthday cake!" said Wendy, excitedly.

When Bob, Scoop and Lofty got to Farmer Pickles' barn, Travis and Spud were already there.

Bob started to pull the old planking off the wall so he could replace it with new planking.

"Pull harder, Bob!" yelled Spud.

"I'm doing my best," grunted Bob. Suddenly the plank came loose and Bob fell back on his bottom. Things weren't going that well for Bob on his birthday!

Back at the yard, Dizzy and Muck watched Wendy make Bob's birthday cake.

"Making a cake looks easy," said Dizzy. "You just throw everything together and mix it up. Just like making concrete!"

"Hey, why don't we make Bob a concrete cake he can keep forever? Can we make it?" asked Muck.

"Yes, we can!" exclaimed Dizzy.

Dizzy whipped up a load of her very best concrete. Then she poured it into a tyre mould. Roley helped Muck and Dizzy decorate their concrete cake with some flowers, feathers, and leaves.

"Wow! Cool cake," Roley said.

At Farmer Pickles' barn, Bob and Lofty were still working hard. Their work was coming along nicely.

"Travis and Spud, aren't you two supposed to be delivering Farmer Pickles' eggs?" asked Bob.

"You're right!" said Travis, starting up his engine. "Come on, Spud," he called. "I'll drop you off at Bob's house."

At Bob's house, Wendy had finished making Bob's birthday cake. "Mmmmmm!" exclaimed Spud, as he scooped some icing off the cake and plopped it into his mouth.

"Spud!" Wendy yelled.

"I'm sorry, Wendy," Spud mumbled. "But it looks so good!"

"Do you want to help me put the candles on the cake?" asked Wendy.

"You bet! Spud's on the job!" he laughed.

As Bob nailed the last plank into Farmer Pickles' barn, his phone rang.

"Maybe this is a birthday phone call," he said hopefully.

It was Wendy. "Hi, Bob," she said. "When are you coming home?"

"Actually, we've just finished and we are on our way," Bob told her.

"Why . . . any special reason?"

"No," Wendy replied. "I've just got a few letters for you to sign. Bye."

"No 'Happy Birthday, Bob'," Bob murmured to himself.

Scoop winked at Lofty. "Come on, Bob. Time to go home!" he said.

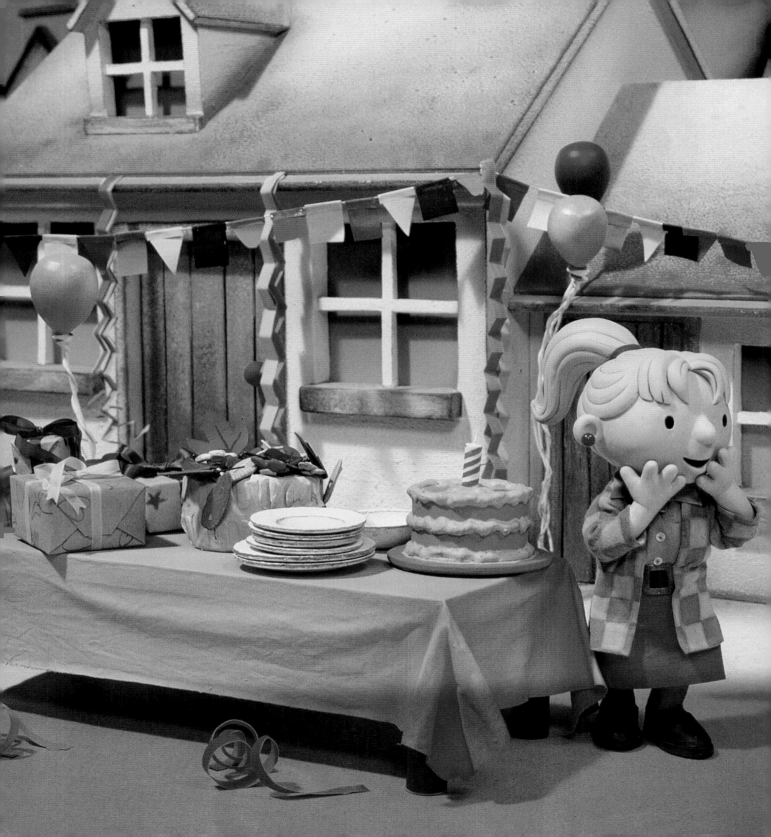

Back at the yard, Wendy, Muck, Dizzy and Roley had decorated a table and covered it with cakes and presents.

Bob couldn't believe his eyes when he arrived.

"Surprise!" laughed Wendy.

"I thought you forgot my birthday!" Bob exclaimed.

"Forget your birthday?" Wendy teased. "Never!"

"Look! You've got two cakes –
a real cake to eat and a concrete
cake you can keep forever!"
said Muck.

Everybody burst out singing:

"Bob the Builder, it's his birthday!
Bob the Builder, yes, it is!

It's Bob's birthday, can we sing it?
It's Bob's birthday – yes, we can!"

"And don't forget your post!" Wendy said.

"Are all these birthday cards for me?" gasped Bob.

"Of course," replied Wendy, "you're the Birthday Builder!" Everyone cheered,

"Hooray!"

"Now can I please have a slice of that scrummy cake?" begged Spud, interrupting.

"Of course you may," said Bob, as he cut Spud a huge piece!

Spud stuffed the piece of cake into his mouth and smiled.

"Like I always say:
Spud's on the job, Bob!"